Michael Whaite
100
CATS

PUFFIN

High cat, Sly cat, hide away shy cat,

leap cat,

sleep cat,

lying around the house . . .

fun cat, **run** cat,

lounging in the **sun** cat,

snooze cat –

whose cat,

looking for a mouse?

Purry cat, furry cat, fast and blurry cat,

Caring cat, sharing cat, stood still staring cat,

Welly cat, smelly cat, eating from the bin . . .

stretch cat, fetch cat, what have you dragged in?

Wussy cat,

fussy cat,

MEOW!

that's
new
Pussy
cat!

Art cat, smart cat,

opening the door . . .

Fish cat,

swish cat,

that is
not your
dish
cat!

Lucky cat,

mucky cat,

messing up the floor.

Kitty cat, pretty cat, streetwise city cat,

Tabby cat, shabby cat, overfed flabby cat,

fright cat, night cat,
see his eyes glow . . .

jewel cat,

COOL CAT

going with the flow.

Spin cat,  **grin** cat,  head stuck in a **tin** cat,

cute cat,

boot cat,

from a fairy tale . . .

Lynx cat, sphynx cat,

having **forty winks** cat,

shed cat, shred cat,

opening your mail.

sitting cat, spitting cat,

tangled in your knitting cat,

paw cat, claw cat,

ruining your chair . . .

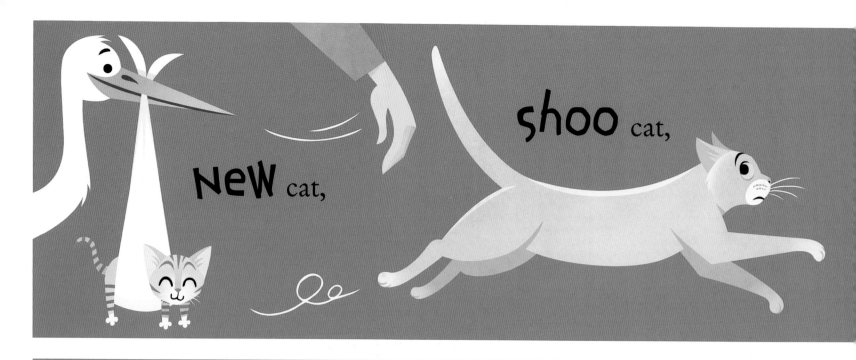

NEW cat,

shoo cat,

living in the ZOO cat,

Meme cat, **Scream** cat, always gets the **cream** cat,

Styled cat, **Wild** cat,

never will be tame . . .

Clean cat, mean cat, visiting the queen cat,

floppy cat, copy cat,

looking just the same!

NOSY cat,

dozy cat,

comfy
and
COSy
cat,
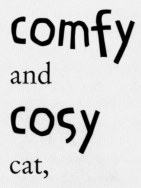

sock cat,

clock cat . . .

TICK! TOCK! TICK!

Groom cat, ZOOOOOOOM cat,

hairless cat,

flying on a **broom** cat,

careless cat –

catch
that,
quick!

Flounce cat, **bounce** cat, wake you with a **Pounce** cat,

rip cat,

ship cat, sailing out to sea . . .

RUB cat, SCRUB cat, get back in the tub cat,

SWIPE cat, stripe cat, calling in for tea.

Bad cat,

sad cat, looking very mad cat,

top cat,

drop cat,

1st

landing on all fours . . .

spray cat, stray cat,

spy cat,

which cat's

PUFFIN BOOKS

UK | USA | Canada | Ireland | Australia
India | New Zealand | South Africa

Puffin Books is part of the Penguin Random House group of companies
whose addresses can be found at global.penguinrandomhouse.com.

www.penguin.co.uk   www.puffin.co.uk   www.ladybird.co.uk

Penguin
Random House
UK

First published 2019
001

Copyright © Michael Whaite, 2019
The moral right of the author has been asserted

Clock cat is based on
Kit-Cat Klock ® by the Calfornia Clock Company,
reproduced here with kind permission

Printed in China
A CIP catalogue record for this book is available from the British Library

ISBN: 978-0-241-34783-6

Did
you spot
my cat?

for
Linda + David